# I'm Not ready to go to bed !

Written by:

Rozzi Osterman

Illustrated by:

Victoria Anderson

# I'm Not Ready To Go To Bed !

This book interprets what a child is feeling
at bedtime.

The rhymes are constructed
to gently transition the child and reader
from busy daily activity to a relaxed state.

The verse and illustrations reflect the stages
of resistance and reluctance to sleepiness,
expressed in concrete thoughts
evolving to images
of fantasy, dreams, and meditation.

This book is designed to facilitate
a shared and calming bedtime experience
for child and reader.

words written cherished
shared images read aloud
imagination journey

haiku by Z. Newman

# Dedication to

my insightful and kindhearted children
&
forever supportive and caring husband
&
Victoria Anderson for generously sharing her gifts

*Sleep is essential for our children's physical and mental health. Youngsters thrive on a healthy routine. A good night's sleep begins with a soothing bedtime ritual. This goal is artfully achieved in this thoughtful book of bedtime lyrics.*

John D. Osterman, MD
Pediatric Neurologist and Father of three

# The Night Has Not Begun

It's been such a great day,
I just want to go and play.
The night has not begun,
we should take more time for fun.

First, I need to ride my bike,
give me time to fly my kite.
I forgot to pull my wagon,
haven't found my favorite dragon.

I will skip and jump and hop,
after spinning like a top.
Try to swing a baseball bat,
someone has to feed the cat.

No one's tired, not my cars,
not even my painting jars.
Not my crayons, not my clay,
so, do not stop my today.

I'm not ready to go to bed,
let's get up and begin instead.
I just want to go and play,
it's been such a great day.

## It's Not Fair

It's not fair,
I want to stay up too.
We can rest awhile,
just me and you.

I know people are awake,
sleeping now is a mistake!

It's not fair,
I want to stay up too.
We can rest awhile,
just me and you.

Even though the sun has set,
kids don't want a bedtime yet!

It's not fair,
I want to stay up too.
We can rest awhile,
just me and you.

## If It Was Simple

I simply could be quiet now
If it was easy to learn how
But my mind keeps me wandering
Filling up with noisy pondering

When I hear loud booming thunder
Is the sky yelling? I do wonder
A wet rainstorm seems like crying
And a rainbow does the drying

A thin string holds up a kite
Only when the wind pulls tight
Hot tea needs a sturdy kettle
Then the water has to settle

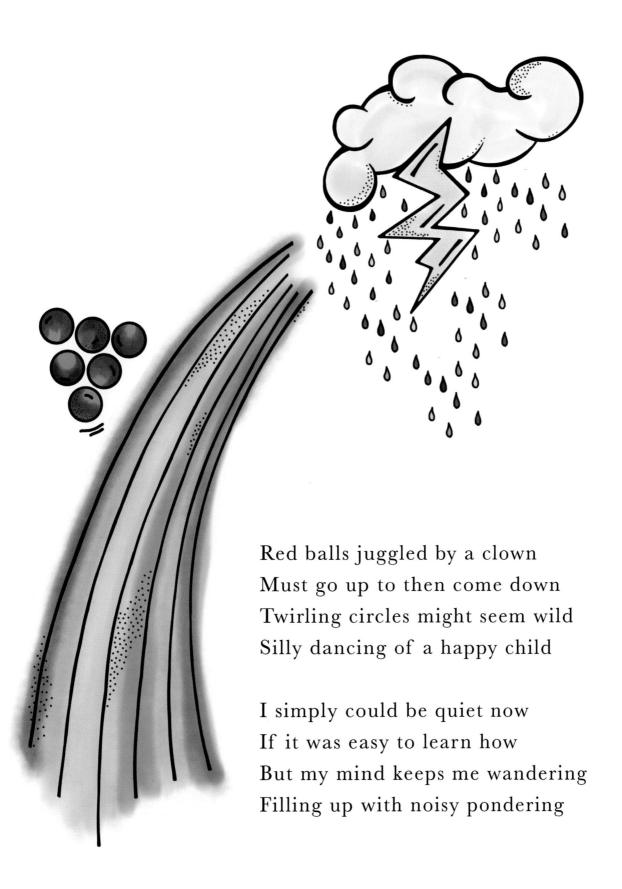

Red balls juggled by a clown
Must go up to then come down
Twirling circles might seem wild
Silly dancing of a happy child

I simply could be quiet now
If it was easy to learn how
But my mind keeps me wandering
Filling up with noisy pondering

## OK, I'm in Bed

OK, I really am in bed
but a butterfly is in my head
together we see new faces
fly away to colorful places

I am soaring up tall heights
mountain greens turn into whites
children sliding down soft hills
snowflakes flurry from their thrills

Winter cold melts into streams
jumping fish with mermaid dreams
silky silver waters flow
flowering meadows almost glow

Warmer air is getting dry
underneath the desert sky
lined like soldiers stand cacti
brave and daring heads held high

Dusty brown turns into blues
ocean tide in rhythm moves
lively surfers splashing fun
big waves laughing at the sun

OK, I really am in bed
but a butterfly is in my head
together we see new faces
fly away to colorful places

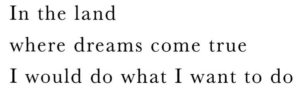

## The Best Place Ever

In the land
where dreams come true
I would do what I want to do

Sing to a spider
and wrestle a frog

Swing on a moonbeam
with a big blue dog

Talk to a rock and tickle a fish
Swim in a fancy serving dish

Climb a canyon of vanilla ice cream
Ride a green feather floating upstream

In the land where dreams come true
I would do what I want to do

What fun I'd have in this perfect place
I'd like to play there

How 'bout you?

# My Pillow And The Clouds

Above my own fluffy pillow
Whipped cream clouds like balloons billow
Before the air lets them escape
I like to guess their floating shape

Can I see a puffy porcupine
Become a face that looks like mine
A cowboy riding topples down
His frown is now a royal crown

Long rows of tiny ducks
Waddle past a fleet of trucks
Bird wings spanning out for miles
Flowers blossom into smiles

A pink cotton candy bear
Resting in a rocking chair
Shaking from a crazy sneeze
Suddenly blowing up a breeze

These clouds must not be tired
They are circling around my bed
Now I need my eyes to rest
And hug the pillow I love best

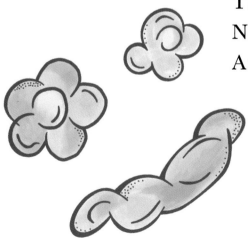

## The Wind And The Tree

Outside just past my window,
the wind is singing with the tree.
In a dark and quiet shadow,
their sweet harmony beckons me.

In a hushed voice, I slowly
whisper amongst we three:
"I'm in bed, so, I can't play,
but I will the very next day."

Tree paints the leaves bright colors and shade,
green, yellow, and red, orange marmalade.

Wind and leaves happily dance,
joyful sway in nature's trance.

Together they shine and shimmer,
swirling streamers golden glimmer.

Outside just past my window,
the wind is singing with the tree.
In a dark and quiet shadow,
gentle harmony beckons me.

In a hushed voice, I slowly
whisper amongst we three:
"I'm in bed, so, I can't play,
but I will the very next day."

# The Stars Very Bright

The sky is so dark
stars sparkling bright
like jewels on a necklace
they shine through the night

My room simply quiet
toy trains standing still
dolls already sleeping
along the windowsill

Pajamas are comfy
the blanket is light
feeling snug and cozy
I'm tucked in just right

Air easy and soothing
as clouds sail away
the moon guards the night
waiting for a new day

The sky is so dark
stars sparkling bright
like jewels on a necklace
they shine through the night

# Relaxation from Head To Toe

deep breath in...

deep breath out...

soft breath in...

soft breath out...

my head
peaceful on my pillow

eyes quiet sweetly rest

my lips
silent in gentle stillness

body calm and content

my arms
drifting down my sides

hands and fingers feather light

my legs
float long and limber

knees
nestle between the sheets

my feet
feel warm and toasty

and my toes
just said good night

sweet dreams
and
sleep tight ...

# Author's Notes

My parents loved to read. They weren't adventurous travelers; we didn't go on many vacations, content at home, they avidly read newspapers, magazines, and books. Together, they learned about developments in the world, exotic places, and diverse cultures.

My father was an encyclopedia of knowledge on subjects ranging from great importance to funny facts. Perhaps, his training as an engineer made it easy for him to explain how underwater tunnels are built and the basics of soda water. He always said that if there is a proper manual, and one can read, one can fix anything.

It is no surprise that my mother liked books, as she taught reading in public schools for over fifty years. In particular, she loved to teach poetry. Our garage never housed cars, but was an elaborate maze of shelves that held lesson plans, teaching games, art supplies, and countless books for children.

In my early twenties, I moved to Israel and lived on a kibbutz, a communal farm. There I met a young man that loved to read; not only did he love to read, but he loved to read aloud. I began to listen to the words of Steinbeck, Faulkner, Hemingway, and even Shakespeare's sonnets.

Together, for many years, we have read aloud to each other and to our children.

It is my deepest wish that these verses are read aloud and enjoyed as a family tradition.

With Love,

*Rozzi Osterman*

Rozzi Newman Osterman

# About the Author

Rozzi Newman Osterman studied music and film at Tel Aviv University and performed as a soprano soloist throughout Israel. She began her career as an Israeli actress on television.

As a writer/director, Ms. Osterman, has created award-winning documentaries on issues about children with special needs and their families. She has worked with many non-profit organizations including The Shoah Foundation. *I'm Not Ready To Go To Bed!* has been a dream project and she is delighted to collaborate with the artist Victoria Anderson.

# About the Illustrator

Victoria Anderson is a graphic artist and marketing consultant. She also manages her daughter's career in Los Angeles, who is an actor/film editor and on the Autism spectrum.

As a producer, she is involved in several web series and small film projects, many of which have won awards.

Along with her husband, Ms. Anderson is bi-coastal, travelling between California and Florida supporting and raising her three children, all who have special needs. She is honored to be asked to work on this beautiful and lyrical book, and pleased for the opportunity to support children's charities.